Bear's New House

By Annie Cobb • Illustrated by Kathy Wilburn

Silver Press

Produced by Chardiet Unlimited, Inc. and Daniel Weiss Associates, Inc.
33 West 17th Street, New York, NY 10011

Educational Consultant:
Dr. Priscilla Lynch

GOING PLACES™ is a trademark of Daniel Weiss Associates, Inc.
and Chardiet Unlimited, Inc.

Published by Silver Press, a division of
Silver Burdett Press, Inc., Simon & Schuster, Inc.
Prentice Hall Bldg., Englewood Cliffs, NJ 07632
For information address: Silver Press.

Printed in the United States of America
10 9 8 7 6 5 4 3 2 1

Library of Congress Cataloging-in-Publication Data

Cobb, Annie
Bear's New House/written by Annie Cobb;
illustrated by Kathy Wilburn
p.   cm.—(Going places)
Summary: Bear's friends understand simple concepts about scale
and measurement when Grampy and Inchworm help them build
a new house for Bear.
1. Going—Juvenile literature. [1. Going] I. Wilburn, Kathy, ill. II.
Title. III. Series: Going places
(Englewood Cliffs, N.J.)

ISBN 0-671-70393-5 (LSB)

ISBN 0-671-70397-8 (trade)

"What took you so long?" called Bear, as
Squirrel came down the path.

Bear had invited Squirrel to sleep over. He had
been waiting by the mailbox all afternoon.

"I had to pack my bag," said Squirrel, as they
walked up to Bear's house. "But before I could
pack my bag..."

"I had to mend my pajamas…"
Bear opened the door.
"But before I could mend my pajamas…Bear!
What are you doing?" cried Squirrel.
Bear seemed to be wedged in the doorway.
"My doorway is too narrow," said Bear, as he
finally squeezed through the door.

Bear began setting out dishes.

"I made some...ow!...acorn...ow!...cookies...
ow!...for you," said Bear.

"Bear! What's the matter?" cried Squirrel.

Bear was bumping his head a lot.

"My ceiling is too low," said Bear, as he
sat down.

That night, after a delicious supper, Bear and
Squirrel went to bed. Squirrel curled up on
the floor in his sleeping bag. Bear stretched out
on his bed.

Squirrel looked up. "Yikes!" he cried. Two big
furry paws were hanging right over his head.

They belonged to Bear.

"My bed is too short," said Bear, as he wiggled
his toes.

The next day Squirrel called all of Bear's
friends together. They met near Beaver Pond.
"Bear has been growing bigger," said Squirrel.
"His house is too small for him now."

"Let's build him a new house," said Porcupine.
"It can be a surprise," said Beaver.
"I hope this doesn't mean work,"
mumbled Raccoon.

They decided to build Bear's new house near Beaver Pond. Everyone pitched in.

Beaver cut boards that were nice and long.

Squirrel cut boards that were nice and short.

Raccoon hammered boards together at one end of the house.

Porcupine hammered boards together at the other end.

Mrs. Rabbit worked on the roof.

The next day Squirrel brought Bear to
Beaver Pond.

"SURPRISE!" shouted Bear's friends.

Bear stared at his new house. Something was
wrong. One end of the house slanted up.
One end of the house slanted down.
The roof zigzagged.

Looking at it made Bear dizzy.

Everyone began to talk at once.

"Beaver, you cut the boards too long,"
said Squirrel.

"Squirrel," said Beaver, "you cut the boards
too short."

"Porcupine, you built the house too low,"
said Raccoon.

"No, Raccoon, you built the house too high,"
said Porcupine.

Just then Grampy came along.

"Uh-oh," said Grampy. "I bet you didn't follow your plan."

Everyone gasped. "PLAN?"

"We don't have a plan," said Squirrel.

"Hmmmm," said Grampy.

"You can't build a house without a plan," explained Grampy.

"Where do we get one?" asked Porcupine.

"You can make one," said Grampy. "A plan is just a picture that shows how big the house is going to be."

"How big do you want your house to be, Bear?" asked Squirrel.

Bear put out his arms. "This big!" he said.

Grampy laughed. "Can you be more exact?"

Bear walked along the ground, heel to toe, counting his steps.

"Twenty bear feet long!" announced Bear. "And twenty bear feet wide!"

"It will have to be smaller," said Squirrel. "We don't have any paper *that* big."

"You don't need a big piece of paper," said Grampy. "You can draw a plan on a small piece of paper. You can draw it *to scale*."

"SCALE?" Everyone gasped again.

Grampy went away and came back with some paper and a tiny little green animal.

"This is Inchworm," said Grampy. "He is going to help us with the scale."

"Hi, everybody!" said Inchworm in a teeny, tiny voice.

"How can a little worm help us build a big house?" asked Raccoon.

"I'll show you," said Grampy.

Inchworm stretched out on the paper and
Grampy drew a line that was just as long
as Inchworm.

"One inchworm will stand for four bear feet,"
said Grampy. Grampy made a picture that said that.
It looked like this:

Grampy drew a picture of a house. It was five *inchworms* long and five *inchworms* wide. But the picture stood for a house that was twenty *bear feet* long and twenty *bear feet* wide.

"Now you have a plan," said Grampy.

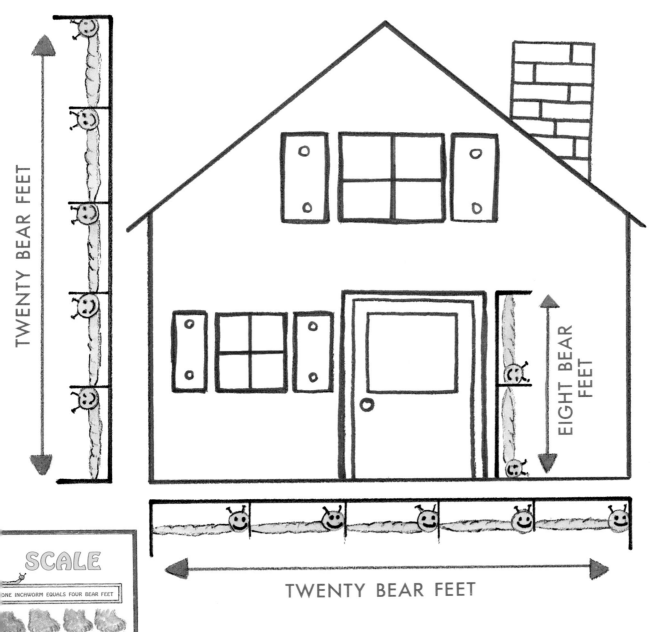

TWENTY BEAR FEET

EIGHT BEAR FEET

TWENTY BEAR FEET

SCALE

ONE INCHWORM EQUALS FOUR BEAR FEET

23

"What about Bear's bed?" asked Grampy. "How long should it be?"

"Longer than Bear!" said Squirrel.

"And what about the door?" asked Grampy. "How wide should it be?"

"Wider than Bear," said Squirrel.

"And what about the ceiling?" asked Grampy. "How high should it be?"

"Higher than bear!" said Squirrel.

Then Grampy measured Bear. He measured Bear's height. He measured Bear's width.

They were ready to begin building.

Beaver and Squirrel cut the boards, according to the plan.

Raccoon and Porcupine hammered the boards, according to the plan.

Mrs. Rabbit worked on the roof, according to the plan.

Bear made himself a bed.

The new house for Bear was finished.

Bear looked at the new house. Everything was right.

It was just the right size.

He could go through the door without getting wedged.

He could set the table without bumping his head.

He could lie down on his bed without his feet hanging off the end.

"Hooray!" said Bear. "Thank you, everyone, for my *wonderful* new house."

Toot, toot!

It was Grampy in his little blue car. And the car was full of Bear's furniture. Porcupine and Beaver had helped Grampy do the moving.

"Surprise!" they shouted.

And as soon as Bear was settled, he had a housewarming party. Everyone came, even Inchworm.

"Thank you, Inchworm, for helping us make a plan," said Squirrel. "We couldn't have built Bear's house without you."

Happy housewarming, Bear!